The Cow that lost its MOOOOOOoo...

Andrea Pincoski

Illustrated by
Kara Storey

Spread Kindness
like Confetti, its
the best way to make
friends
xo
Andrea Pk

Book Vine Press
2516 Highland Dr.
Palatine, IL 60067

Dedication

Dedicated to my husband Justin,
for the encouragement.

To my children, Zora, Justin Jr., and Olive, for
all the imagination you've given to me.

To Kara Storey for her fantastic illustrations that
bring this story to life! And last but most definitely
not least; To all our farmer family & friends
that brave our four Western New York seasons
keeping the herds happy, and produce fresh!

I bought a cow, a happy cow,

a cow that sang a song.

He sang and sang.

One day he stopped.

I said, "Poor cow what's wrong?"

I thought and thought, what could it
be to make my poor cow moo?

I drove and drove

and then I stopped.
I knew just what to do.

I drove as fast as I could go, it must have been ten miles.

I drove to many nearby farms,
and then I had a big smile!

When my cow saw his cow friend, he
started singing loud and clear!

The two friends sang all night long,
and happiness filled the air.